FAR COUNTRY

Far Country

Poems

KYCE BELLO

UNIVERSITY OF NEVADA PRESS | Reno & Las Vegas

University of Nevada Press | Reno, Nevada 89557 USA
www.unpress.nevada.edu
Copyright © 2024 by University of Nevada Press
All rights reserved

Manufactured in the United States of America

FIRST PRINTING

Cover design by Caroline Dickens
Cover art: Bardsey Boats © Jake Lever

Library of Congress Cataloging-in-Publication Data
Names: Bello, Avtar Kyce, 1981– author.
Title: Far country : poems / Kyce Bello.
Description: First edition. | Reno, Nevada USA : University of
    Nevada Press, 2025.
Summary: "In her new collection, Far Country, Kyce Bello docu-
    ments an unmapped territory in which loss becomes a medium
    for deepening connection and love. In poems firmly rooted in
    the Southwestern bioregion, landscape and language are layered
    into vivid sequences where the personal, collective, and ecological
    merge and illuminate one another"—Provided by publisher.
Identifiers: LCCN 2024032120 | ISBN 9781647791810 (paperback)
    | ISBN 9781647791827 (ebook)
Subjects: LCGFT: Poetry.
Classification: LCC PS3602.E4584 F37 2025 | DDC 811/.6—dc23/
    eng/20240719
LC record available at https://lccn.loc.gov/2024032120

ISBN 9781647791810 (paper)
ISBN 9781647791827 (ebook)
LCCN: 2024032120

Contents

FAR COUNTRY

Blood City

The city of blood has fallen asleep.
Children play tag on bones,
runners jog over bones, but no one knows
bones are underfoot. Women fill grocery carts
with bread and buy drive-thru coffee
as if the grass they stand upon
never buried a past, let alone a people.
I lived in those places once, but came home.
Here, watchmen peer from towers, eyes
set on the red horizon. We have what other
places call history, but we call bodies.
The stones on the trail are really snakes,
coiled stiff as fossils. They are not dead
but dormant. The stones underfoot are eggs,
strong as marble. What have snakes
to do with bones? Better to ask
what these bones will hatch, what lies,
curled, inside the shells of the dead.

Triptych in Which My Firstborn Reads Percy Jackson Every Night Before Bed

1.

What is Jupiter the god of again? she hollers.
I can't recall. But here is something handy
I learned as a child—never wear rings
on your middle finger, your Saturn finger,
because Saturn already has rings.
I can't remember what Saturn is the god of, either,
but Susie McCall used to shout *Fuck you,*
Saturn! when bills were due, when pipes burst,
when her boyfriends slept with her friends,
so maybe something to do with patriarchy.
Susie wore silver and taught me to harvest roots
when the moon passed through Virgo,
to turn weeds into blood tonic and love potion.
She taught me to kindle logs and start fires
in the woodstove. Has the earth gone too quiet
in my hands? Of course I recognize myself
these days. It just looks like someone else.

2.

Still reading Greek Myths.
  Still have a jar of *Anemopsis* roots

dug from the marsh along the San Pedro River,
  may she rest in peace.

Still planning a garden, no matter
  how much water it wants.

Still thanking the dead poet for her lines.
  Still asking God for lines of my own.

Which god grants that, again?
  Still dusting, still watching dust motes in the sun.

Still trying new words, still erasing.
  Still taking the auspices.

Still cross myself when crossing rivers,
  especially dry ones.

3.

On the banks of a river that is now a ghost,
          an herbalist plucks yerba mansa leaves
     so we might taste bitter medicine,

and we have our first kiss soon after.
          Our eyes glow like candles
     lit and whispered over,

while our hands meet like a prayer
          greeting the unknown, spoken
     in the unknown's mother tongue.

Mornings, I set out into the field
          to watch the steadiness with which we move
     toward grief. Maps show none

of these rutted roads crossing
          the open desert, nor the thresholds
     we pass through, unadorned by belief.

Walk in the Nambé Badlands

Each landmark a story of times women walked here.

Dried grasses waver over cold ground,
>and a path emerges between golden stems.

>>It is snowing and I cannot find the door that opens into a
>>warm room.

Snakebroom and saltbush collect drifts in their dried blooms.

There is a well in the center
>of my chest out of which I cannot drink.

>>If there is a lantern in my hand,
>>>it bears a flickering light,

and if there is a map that can guide me,
>it was erased in the last brief rain.

Night Being a Moonlit Ordeal

Someone is always coming in the door,
leaving the door open, letting

the horses out the door to cross night swiftly.
Night being a moonlit ordeal

where we gather salt in an ocean-licking mist,
where beautiful words are spoken

as if they are honey, and the tongue an apple
peeled and sliced to eat.

By beautiful you can see I mean the words
are not sweetness, but two parts wild spinach seed

soaked in three parts cultured milk. I drove
my truck up the plateau to be noticed,

but instead took notice of those I did not know.
It makes me feel both important and lonely,

like dream after dream of men begging me
to love them and to take hold of long grasses

with my hands. Our fortunes rise in small parts
over the horizon, and someone asks,

Is it day? Where is the light?

Balsamic Moon

We live south of the future, where the ground

tilts toward winter. The reduction season calls us

to our rest, our cure. The mountains turn shaggy

with grasses, their flanks overgrown with graves.

Once each month, a sliver of moon hangs

in the eastern sky like an empty bowl that rises at dawn

and fades with first light. Our bodies move uphill

the way fingers move knots on the prayer rope.

Each day ends sooner than the one before.

We circle and wait for the fire to burn low,

but the coals last all night. We comb the hills

for medicine, the winter sun setting on our backs.

Field Apothecary

Morning baskets
mullein leaves into bundles

The light in the meadow a door left open
from winter

     That is

lady slipper in bloom
under aspens

slick logs yielding the creek

*

I have bottled for myself
the wet root crossing

     Long chains of asters pierced
and threaded into a crown

*

One wound

     or another
Dressed and left to heal
     How promising the forest becomes

     How helpful wild things

     How useful to remember their names

*

Forever naming and naming plants
Until they become

Medicine chest composed of light on leaves

      Western / swamp / field / privet

Cattails and thistles fill the low field, the marsh

      Yerba / yerba / yerba

Certain things are remembered and put into the basket

      mother / silver / lesser / western

Long grass in the long light

      wort / leaf / root / herb / seed

*

Sunflowers wave their hundred gold crowned heads

*

see the salve made from flowers   steeped in simple oil

      infused in the sun   strained through cloth

      the oil gold green as it cascades

      stainless steel bowl rimmed

      in precious droplets   and the oil warmed just so with
        beeswax

little jars filled   and now my hands rub salve

into your wounds   little named one   be still and
    let me help you

*

I was again asked about my name

I'd like to just to say it is my own prefix
I don't know the end of

I name each leaf, each twig, each petal

All of it gathered in hand
until I become suffix

        until

the meadow overlaps in verbs

to yarrow / to verbena / to mint / to wort / to silver / to weed

*

I place them all in my basket

Remedy upon remedy
in hand

gathered according to that old way
    we have of always looking back

though we stand
upright in the field

*

The first prophecies

        made by women
        involved bloodstains

So many bewilder-
ments to sort out

by spilling

*

        Can you tell
        what these
        shadow-
        puppets spell

in the alphabet

of hands
held up
to lamplight

or is it just me reading darkness as it dances on the wall?

*

        Story telling indeed

*

There are so many shadows just outside
the bright circle we make

This is what is meant
                    by balm
by salve
        by fragrant poultice

                see how the field
                brims with remedies

*

little summer moths

little autumn leaves

little dandelion fluffs held to my lips

                bitter bright medicine

I have tasted each one

*

Where the stream disappears
            into long grasses

and cold ground dips
            into hollows

we go on gathering till morning

Walk in the Nambé Badlands
Where the Midwife Walked

One winter, the midwife lost her footing and fell
                off a small cliff at the edge of the badlands.

She spent the night injured, frostbitten and alone
until three roaming dogs

            found her and stayed by her side. Help arrives
in all its faces,
        most of them unseen and ignored.

Try the spell, the incantation, the plea.

The contours of particular sorrows not unlike these undulations
            of erosion
                and disassembly,

this landscape crossed and crossed again
            by the circular path searching takes.

The Search for the Golden Spike

Not to be obscure, but take recent fallout

        recorded in stone.

      Human generated deposits

         held in watery fields, in estuary & peat bog,

even biological hosts:

        coral & trees,

      children—they wake

        every morning about this time.

Unprecedented accuracy. Birdsong.

         The best spike left by plutonium bomb tests,

      sampled in marine & lake sediment,

        ice layers, perhaps even speleothems.

Scientists conclude they are nearing agreement.

        Set in motion up the valley—

Conifers, contour.

        It doesn't take long for morning to lift

a thin layer of mist from the grass it beds against.

        It doesn't take long.

        Just now it happened.

Loss is Magnified From Knowing Change

The smell of willow
  of low water and storms

takes hold of memory and body

too late for what we knew—

  trees and streams and birdsong and

          ∧∧   ∧

Cascading losses hang
    between the past

    (sweet cicely bracken fern betony baneberry elderberry mahonia)

    and the vertigo of desecration

    (moss monarda poléo harebell potentilla)

      ∧∧   ∧∧

Large shifts at unprecedented rates
    one could say

all that has named us and all we have named

              all places
    in motion—

we cannot expect the smell of ponderosa to fill every afternoon
    with sweetness

    not every meadow can forever
    have a deer browsing amidst penstemon

and angled sunbeams signaling golden sundown

                 ^^   ^

In all of this there is room for grief—

     the forest we knew becomes the forest we have never seen before

          taking with it lush stands of purple bee balm
            covered in orange butterflies

creek banked in coneflower and ferns
       twinberries gleaming with dew

edging us against
       places we did not seek but have entered

             ^^   ^   ^^

                     Though I summon
my children to the headwaters

     they do not know what it is
they will never see

             ^^   ^   ^

The forest gives way to bones

      and still

coyotes howl from the hollows

still

     mushrooms erupt at sunrise
      just as it begins to rain

In the Future There Will Be No Hospitals

No cities, nor trees. No ruins to house us.

We will die then as we die now.
> Our sick will be given stories

> as remedies, and we will argue with blood

using only thread and yarrow leaf.
> There will be pain,

as there is pain now. We will learn

> what shepherds long ago learned—
how to wait beside a goat in troubled labor,

> her moans neither argued with or silenced.

We will sit on our hands in the darkness
> until whatever needs to be born,

still-bodied or breathing, is born.

> Our healers will travel from the old halls,
where we once tended every sickness with sickness,

> to the new, circular with justice.

We will know the name
> of even the smallest child.

Walk in the Nambé Badlands
Where There is a House

The task to find a place where the land's bones
        become the house
                where a woman labors in a tub by the fire.

She looks down
        at the midwife's bare feet and sees seven missing toes.

When a red-haired boy is born,
            the woman lifts him from the water to her chest.

        We travel these badlands between the cave
            where we drew first breath

and the cave where we will take our last sip from a dark, brimming
    bowl.

        At each crossroad we leave a part of ourselves in offering.

        There is no wind.

The sun is bright today, if cold. Stillness settles in, and takes hold.

The Thin Line

In an encampment in the forest, a hunter
knapping arrowheads says, *There is a hole
where elders used to be.* The thin line
of honking birds overhead could be geese,
but are Sandhill cranes, and I gauge whom
to trust by who can tell the difference.
At their compound, the hunters sleep under
bark and pine boughs. They don't have zippers
or guns. They say that needing each other
and being needed is better even than a grocery store.
At night, they hold hands beneath the black cauldron
swirling milky stars and think
how once each was named, and how now,
or sometime soon enough, when we've forgotten
what to call them, they can be named again.
They dream upon fern beds that soften the night.
One hears rocks singing. One sees a deer turning
its head in the rising mist. One follows.

(

Far Country

Mist snakes the mountains,

uncoiled, unhurried.

> The moon waxes and wanes.

> Storms
> > sometimes never come,

sometimes never go.

There by the creek, there is ice
> > and beneath ice,
chilly pools that heal us.

I send falcons to hunt
         the far watershed.

They dip overland,

return with key after key
clamped in their beaks.

No! I shout. *Bring food!*

Another bit of metal clatters to my feet.

Dry soil softens
between my lips. My mouth deepens

into a well filled with roots.

Inside the door, I hang keys from a nail.

In my cup, bitter leaves.

        If this happened to us or long ago

or is someday going to happen,

I cannot say.

I drink tea brewed from last summer's flowers.

        Petals re-open
    in the pot before pouring.

The ditch fat with runoff,

      snowmelt

           un-dressing granite,
icing my hands into hooks.

      Call it a life, this cloak intended for our backs.

        On the dunes,
every step shifts the surface.

We sink a little even as we climb.

        All this reaching for a resting place
we likely passed years ago.

Feral apple trees

        scattered in the foothills

bloom late

    but still succumb

to a final frost,

nectar hardening
as a gale carries white petals

to the ground.

First *Corydalis* in bloom, sprinkled like
        yellow coins on the forest floor.

First glimpse of the watershed.

First of the fires,
        first un-controlled plume.

First of the elm seeds scattering.

First wait for rain.

First startled memory taking hold. First
        impressions slipping between gaps.

First apricots fattening. First nettle soup to tonic the blood.

First warbler in the apricot tree, first yellow wing. First time

        I told you I loved you.

First word spoken in the morning. First light on the mountain.

Tanagers turn north again.

The usual springtime appearances:

a fresh-laid egg,

thin green spears

       and curled leaves

erupting from bare soil.

Key witness tells some stories but not others

Key holder though the house remains unlocked

Key maker who made this morning who opened this day

Key finder with black wings curved beak talon grasp

Key dream interpreter whose wand is a walking stick

Key to the stars meaning able to travel long distances

Key for waiting for the day when kingdom keys

Another thread unwinds.

Meadow grass ripples
          as if it were a pelt we could run

      our hands through,

          or a creature coming down from the forest
to drink in the semi-dark.

At the creek,
          pools open
      one into the next
          into the next,

and three mule deer lower their heads to drink.

The Bend

Consider the bends in the mountain road
we traveled to reach here, the elderberry thicket
hiding spring-water seeps, or those voices heeded
since childhood with their insistent whisper: *carry on.*
Carrying being by no means the smallest part
of what we are asked to do with our despair.
I don't know what to do about hope. I don't wager
with longing, nor miracles. I am mostly afraid.
I'd rather not watch the forest give way. I like
who I am and who I am loves these mountains
as they are—dense with mortal pine and spruce.
Women gather around a bonfire and the eldest
asks *how do we survive this?* Sparks fly and ash
falls on our heads. Consider the midrash
about how when Pharaoh decreed their firstborn
sons die, the Hebrew men panicked. They divorced
their wives, turned celibate, did anything to evade
the loss of their unborn. Consider that the Hebrew women
answered Pharaoh's threat and their husband's fear
by carrying spicy soup to the fields, anointing their
men in oil, luring them behind bushes. I don't think
it was *hope* that their sons would survive that led them
to seduction, but unyielding obedience to life.
I have abandoned logic before and will do so again.
Consider the bend. I never see it coming.

Because Envy Leads Us
Where We Need to Go

I take the longest route home. Cave creek
to Truchas pass, through the graveyard
forest once burnt, now fallen. I give
birth to three children, all boys. No, all girls.
They look just like me, only unblemished.
I follow those who have what ought to be mine—
the indigo dress, the scarlet bouquet. At dawn
the valley fills with mist, and I sear my way
toward an ending in which I safely arrive.
My house is trimmed in yellow, surrounded
by cherry trees. In each ripe cherry squirms
a single white worm. When the road splits
I always go right. I don't envy those who turn
left. Nobody down that way plays the fiddle.
Nobody there makes pie worth a damn.

Walk in the Nambé Badlands
Where Three Dogs Walk

Caves speckle the *barrancas,* and not one of them has a door.

Each gnarl and twisted branch is a doorknob
                    that leads to the unseen,

but cannot be turned and will not open.
Three dogs walk with their noses on the trail,

alive to the scent of a woman who passed the same distance
                some hours, some days, before.

Perhaps she wasn't here at all. Perhaps she is already gone, her
   injuries

being tended, or perhaps they have healed and years have passed
and she is delivering my friend's baby, or my own.

Or perhaps she has just fallen, and the dogs will smell her first,

then hear her—
                crying or calling or silent—

and go to her side, where they will stay.

Departure

My daughter arrives at a season

　　　　when her eyes

　　turn to two gates swinging open.
On the other side is a boreal forest,

　　　　overgrown but not yet ignited.
Not yet cinders floating

　　　down upon a firstborn's
　　orchard christening.

We toasted the infant's future with ashes in our hair.
　　　　That was the summer

　　our breasts leaked milk
　　　　and we found ourselves inexplicably sad.

I'd linger there, but my daughter departs
　　for the unknown country

　　　　written about in psalms
　　　and scorched by time.

　　I've found a map for her to carry:
All the places water is buried.

Every possible fate awaits her underground,
　　　　and everything she touches

　　will turn to something else.
The phone in her pocket plays a song

I have never heard before,
She holds wheat, a wishbone.

She parts the thorny, berry-laced thicket
and steps through.

Boneyard

1. Descent

For my daughter reads the epigraph, *who wants to—*

Pockets emptied by wind &

        open windowed datura beckoning
moths
    from

        from words I still seek &

cold pebbles & wet grass & from
what place is this?

      The river so much bigger

      than what we have seen &

what is it to not have & to never have known *river* & to arrive in
  the evacuated night

      at these hungry banks?

2. Guard Dogs

If the words were easy to set down

If my daughters were not lost to me as they grew into something
kin to me

If I'd known the way here

If they read the directions scratched on the door

If someone had told me I would survive

If I could break the surface when the river releases me from its
undercurrents

If I had something to smoke right now

If my cards revealed any of what is to come

If Saturn would god damn set already

If you could hold your tongue, husband, and *just not say it*

If my own mother had been told by her mother

3. Rio Abajo Rio

I've been talking of hunger, but only the moon
is full. You stopped eating years ago, and I
soon after. As for drink, this river teems
with plankton but by all means drink.
Gold carp are the only hope we have for finding
the small door *abajo,* but when it opens
I have no map for the labyrinth therein.
My phone gives directions to six beaches
famed for bioluminescence. I feed its maps
to the volcano at Arenal, to the mud geyser
in Yellowstone. Antidote after antidote to despair
blankets the night, but like you, I mistake
them for poison. They crisscross each other
like the Milky Way pouring across the ecliptic.
It is when I reach the X in the road that I arrive.

4. Cicada Medicine

Most of you with grown offspring
    will be unsurprised

by what happens next.
    My daughter

growing and the shell
    she must break out of

is the exoskeleton of my mothering.
    It does not slip off,

but requires relentless force.
    Like that I enter

the stage of the life-cycle
    known as *husk.*

No alarms sound. It is darker
    every morning,

and we sleep a little
    later. At noon,

there is a die-in downtown.
    I care, but since I became

a dried slip of crackling fiber,
    I am more likely

to be blown away
    than ignited.

Which is good since she
    sets fire to me every day.

5. WALK IN DARKNESS

I don't have the map. I don't have the book,
the key, or the cup. I have a blanket,

and wrap it around our shoulders. Day after day
wounds are opened and cleansed,

dressed in fresh gauze. In another life
I was hers and she was mine.

She held my hand and hem. We stretch
our arms each morning upon waking,

reaching not to grasp something
but to practice bending.

I'm asked again what salve to spread
on the arm, the face, the bleeding heart,

but all I remember from past lives
are plagues, not cures.

6. A Familiar Tale

I am Demeter day after day. Wintered, wailing. My daughter is here beside me, but plunges again and again into the well. She calls for me from the bottom, voice thin and far off. I pull her up and hold her to me. After a pause, we resume the fight over her messy room, her homework. To tend a child's despair, Adrie says, do what you have always done: hold, laugh, fight back, go outside, make things. I want to abandon her to the cold and go running under the yellow cottonwoods along the river. She will not go with me. I will not leave her. Demeter grieved her daughter's abduction, yet it was only in Hades that Kore's name could change from *girl* to Persephone. That she could become a goddess in her own right. That she could someday return and teach her mother the mysteries of the dead. My daughter's name appears on prayer lists near and far. Her middle name is Aralia, Latin for spikenard, which Christ was anointed with before the crucifixion and which grows in great clusters along Rio en Medio and almost nowhere else in these mountains. Its berries are dark and spicy. Leah says, be firm but flexible. Unyielding. Strong. How far can I yield? To what do I bend? I bow to it all.

7. Chart of Relevant Geography of Earth and Underworld

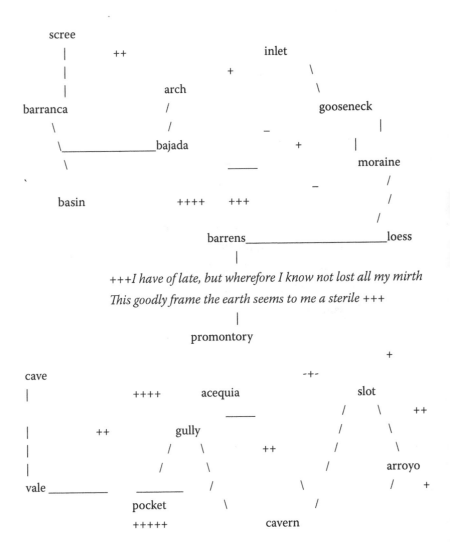

```
scree
  |           ++                        inlet
  |                          +                    \
  |                  arch                          \
barranca                 /                          gooseneck
     \                  /              _                       |
      _____bajada                   +            |
       \                                 _____              moraine
 `                                                  _          /
      basin            ++++    +++                            /
                                                             /
                      barrens_____loess
                          |
```

+++I have of late, but wherefore I know not lost all my mirth
This goodly frame the earth seems to me a sterile +++

```
                          |
                    promontory
                                                      +
cave                                   -+-
  |        ++++        acequia                slot
  |                     _____            /    \       ++
  |          ++     gully              /      \
  |                  /   \      ++    /        \
  |                 /     \          /          arroyo
vale _____   _____  /          \         /    +
            pocket      \              /
            +++++            cavern
```

8. On the Way to Eleusis

I find you ablaze in a small pyre
under the apple tree, eyes dilated
and belly empty. You haven't eaten
in days, and I lift rose petal bread
to your lips. Our temple must not be built
of your bones, but your name has changed,
and I have turned the earth barren with salt.
A team of red mares carries us over
volcanoes. At the southern shore, we bathe
at sunrise, sea foam washing ash from our
breasts and thighs, but it is your own recipe
for visions that restores you, not my pleading
prayers. You open your mouth and spit
raw coals into a clay bowl. I spill them
in my hands, skin blistered and healed
by the same unyielding fire.

9. Prima Materia

The need for fire. The idea of hunger
and its twin: the pain of it. The knowledge of burning,

and the burning.
       The idea of all shall be well

and all shall be well and all manner of things—

of the life you didn't want to live
       coming and becoming, at last, a friend.

Instinct, I hear you at the door. I don't ask the right questions,

       but have you not heard me pleading for answers?
Some clue of how to survive this?

There is no door, no map, no blanket, no pen, no word.

       No more than a bundle of yarrow
in my hands, no more.

10. MOONRISE

The full moon rises and rewinds,

        rises and rewinds, as I drive east on a winter night.

                                         O

∧∧∧∧∧∧∧ O ∧∧∧∧∧∧∧∧   ∧∧∧∧∧∧∧∧∧   ∧∧∧

The full moon pulled down behind the mountains as I drive closer,

        then rising, then falling back

      O   O

∧∧∧∧   ∧∧∧∧∧ ∧ ∧   ∧∧∧∧O∧∧∧   ∧∧∧∧∧ ∧∧∧∧∧∧ ∧∧

        then rising once and for all

       O

∧∧∧∧∧∧   ∧∧∧∧   ∧∧

                                O

                ∧∧∧   ∧∧∧∧∧∧∧∧∧   ∧∧∧∧∧∧.

Walk in the Nambé Badlands Where I Learn

To become mother

To become lost

To be wounded

To become a healer

To become a hunter

To be a bowl

To build the fire

To become a guide

To be guided

To be lost in prayer

To hunger

To become faithful

To become an answer

To become badland

To storm

To be uncertain

To become a key and to turn

Repurposing

We are quarantined by January's overwhelming white
and have vertigo because the snow is the same color
as the fog and we can't see our feet. It becomes a spectacle,
trying to find which way points which way.
We make other mistakes. The twins are born,
and nobody stitches hats for their tiny wrinkled heads.
At least we have radishes to sliver into moons and lay,
burning, on the tongue. The last words I spoke
were slurred the way lace meshes fabric into dainty
but unbreakable bolts of cloth. We make a dozen jackets
and hand them out to men at stoplights.
Reach our hands into the mist and feel them
grow lighter as the heavy garments are lifted
by invisible hands attached to people we cannot see.
That night at the Zen center, the haiku master draws a blank
when composing a verse that includes the season-word *snow*,
tells us instead about a nun who cradled a turnip in her hand
and thought of dead babies. The questioner should begin
where the poet leaves off: How do we write new myths?
Or perhaps, shall we trust death to be its own birth?
After the Dharma talk, a crescent moon hangs in the west
like a parenthesis enclosing a phrase too long to see the end of.
We are high enough up the mountain for winter to pierce
the coat I thought sufficed. I had forgotten what cold feels like,
so thick are the walls were I live, so insulated the windows.

Midwinter Reckoning

In their mineshaft, bats wake from deep torpor
to sip drops of condensation off winter pelts.

The dark is quiet as the space in my chest before candles
are lit, the space out of which I fly on satin wings

when some alarm in my belly says rise, and lights
click on. I no longer know how to pretend I know

what to do. Opossums watched the dinosaurs
die, and they don't seem to mind watching us.

They sacrifice bits of tail and ear to freezing nights,
to the hunger that sends them, scattershot, into snow.

I am bankrupt beneath Venus, lamp bright out the window
as she circles our marriages, our children, our sleep.

Our lives are adorned in stars, and the web of invisible lines
that fashion them into stories. I've told this one

a hundred times but still don't know the end. This ground,
cold and winter fallowed, is a face. It has an eye,

open and unblinking. We study each other as day breaks.

Offering in the Name of the Dead

I can write of the ground and the deep hole opened
in it. I can write of my grandmother's death, but not
my own. After three days she is placed, rose petals
scattered across her body, inside the desert. The moon
crosses the sky. The sun crosses the sky. Sometimes,
both cross together, as happens, also, over the living.
What she held true, I cannot adopt or claim,
even if I agree to its limits, which I do, for I do not
know its edges or belly, its eyelids and fingertips.
I thought humility would help me believe, but am
scolded for credulousness. My faith is a vagrant
that returns winter after winter, drawing closer
to the fire every time. I keep each "truth" I find
in a bowl by the bed so I might begin and end
each day by tasting it. Time will tell if it nourishes
or leaves me hungry. I am alone in the quiet,
my thoughts blazoning the inner chamber. That is,
they armor and unveil me both. This is the narrow
perch from which I witness departure and ripen
toward my own, and yours. This being the waiting
room in which I dedicate psalms to my dead.
There in the newly opened earth, we plant her.

We Planned a Party When
Our Hearts Were Broken

Because the moon is full and it is spring.
Because lilacs, because willows.
Because the river rushes out of the mountains.
Because laughter—we remember that sound.
Because singing.
Because the bowls we set under the stars to collect light
      are overflowing with quicksilver.
Because our eyes rained tears all through the dark winter
      and our faces have thawed like the earth has thawed.
Because it is time to turn soil and plant seeds.
Because the prayers are made
      and might never be answered in any other way.
Because this blooming is the answer,
      and company in the night, and the bell ringing,
      and the egg cracking open,
      and the feast beginning.
Because there are ribbons and flowers to weave into crowns.
Because the thorns need company;
      they do not like to always be naked and alone.

Walk in the Nambé Badlands
When Snow Begins to Fall

Snow meets the earth, hiding the path, my tracks,
the scent of where I stand in the story.

The landscape a crinkled page,
                    and these footprints
first to write everything I have spoken.

            Dreams raise strangeness from the depths
            and give it to us for company.

The snake with wings,
            the charging bull with no back legs,

the oddness that prophesies and opens the way
            for what shall happen next.

Like keys that have not yet found a lock,
            or these many locks

            for which there is no key
and these doors behind which there is no room.

The sky is heavy overhead,
a third house with open windows.

Almanac with Ephemeral River

1. THE RIVER OPENS ITS BRANCHES

At dawn the crescent moon, crowned
by Mars & Jupiter, hangs in the pale sky
like a steer head with two dazzling horns.
Celestial bodies circle day and night.
Their wide net, shifting by degree,
catches us in the form of mood and fortune.
This Pluto phase is going to be difficult,
we tell each other, or overhear. Night has its own
silhouette, its own tree limbs against sky,
its own unseen raccoons—but so do I.
My breasts grow heavy when the moon wanes.
My dreams are all wells and ditches, streams
running over while each of us waits
like a bell in the tower, untouched by even
the slightest wind. The river dries into a corridor
of willow leaves gilded yellow.
When flowers are needed, I remember the weeds
overtaking the parked car: globemallow
and purple aster cut just as first frost looms.

2. Ritual With Half Remembered Song

A jogger glances over her shoulder,
alert to cougars that might collide

with her as she weaves between ponderosas
adorned in brown needles. At first

she fears the entire mountain is dying,
then remembers molting

is part of the life cycle of a pine.
What to cry for becomes *What to let go of.*

Beneath a bower of piñons,
four women watch the half moon

rise in Libra. When they start singing,
they remember nearly all the words.

One looks at the night sky
from inside the weft of pine needles,

sees that their bodies are threads
strung upon a loom. The refrain

catches them, carries them
to the next verse. As the moon glides

higher, shadows narrow underfoot.

3. Windows

The Sagittarian moon rises over Matachines dancers in the
    Santuario parking lot

Marriage too, an emptied riverbed

Too many tears to drink

Other points of view go ignored

Baby boy is named Fox in his father's language

Four candles in the dark room

One hand holds a cross and one hand holds a circle

Bead after bead after bead after bead

This could be a crown or it could be a flower

Something to do with futility

A third death takes place and two more wait in the folds

4. News of the World

Worst drought in 1200 years is confirmed.
The farmer leaves her husband

at the time when ordinarily she would sow seeds
in the star-studded ground.

The river rushes snowmelt, then dwindles.
When the feast of San Isidro arrives,

villagers process to its banks and turn the water
red with roses. It runs dry soon after.

I run into the weeds, the willows, the rocks,
feet steady as the sun's relentless glare.

My prayer forgets if it should ask
for some good outcome, some relief, or accept reality

as it is, and so becomes *mercy, mercy, mercy.*

5. Glossary

refrain | breath returns us to breath time after time

glance | aspen trunks covered in wounds resembling wide open eyes

look | but take into account the unseen

river | another way to be anointed

marriage | the apples were eaten as quickly as they fell

molt | I heard on the first try what you said before you spoke

mercy | the house I make my way towards

dawn | fire leaves us warm but still hungry

loom | or is it a lyre with strings set upon a frame?

crown | doctrine holds the divine encompasses the material world

collide | a list of meeting places begins and ends with river

6. TRAVELERS

We turn lights off to lure
        Miller moths outside toward streetlamps
and stars. For two weeks in May,

        when we walk under cottonwoods,
the canopy implodes with their tiny bodies—
        winged, furred, and constellating

in frenzied forms. They leave moisture
        on our cheeks and arms when they brush us.
As if we wept, as if it rained.

        They are not from here and will not stay.
The river, too, is gone.
        It is our bodies that it runs through

when it is taken from the ground,
        our bodies that become riverbeds.
Other things run dry. Do I forget God

        or does God forget me?
Drink after drink of river the only prayer
        I remember, manage, make.

7. CATALOG OF MYSTERIES

Another tally of dead trees

All sense of perspective muted by a-historicity

We do not age well

Even dreams become deliveries we refuse

Water fills the dry ditch as we step over

Someone is pregnant

There is a baby inside that blood

Songs are debated before they are sung

"My innumerable hands, the weight I bear with all of my arms"

River turned off on Saturday: we do that now

The forest not meant to signal beyond its being

No one knows what anyone knew before us

Somehow we know this

8. ALL THAT CAN BE SEEN IS SEEN

with line by Meister Eckhart

At the oxbow, you abandon creek,
       meadow, even dank mud

      where feet crater grass
into small, pocked pools.

What verb shall you use
      for "astronomer"? Stargaze?

Astron? Look? When you step
        out to observe the night,

      you peer into a veil
of apple leaves, cricket songs, sirens.

      *God is at home, and we
are in the far country.* Another bend

becomes an island as the river
       tightens around it.

9. New Moon in Cancer

A chainsaw whirls its blade into dead wood:
the forest in which we live. It speaks its forgotten
language in pine scent, in stacking, in fire.
What it says depends on last night's dream.
Vigil after vigil, and still the need for something
more and *soon* overwhelms me. When light
falls through an arched window an hour before
vespers, the icon is lit just so. It *becomes* vespers,
that is, the west, evening, prayer, light.
Wildfire smoke thickens and sends us indoors,
where we hear, for the first time this year, a cricket
scrape its leg against its wing. Not far from here,
women massage roses with their hands, dissolving
petals into a bowl of water. They dip fingers
into rose water, sprinkle it on one another's
heads. We imagine it is so. We listen until it is.

10. The Summer of Lost Things

Lakes empty into rivers,

into the river whose light I do not believe
even as it rises and falls

      and falters open.

We wade into shallows,
      call to the children

we once towed behind us
in their own small crafts

during the long years of walking.

Eventually we arrived
      to the decade of the unimagined self

married to the unimagined spouse.
What life is this?

I call to my unimagined daughters.
Their bodies lengthening, their hair tangled,

their gazes fixed
      on green-gold ripples
sequined in sun.

11. GLOSSARY

lure | for my name is being called in the distance

implode | the opening after the unthinkable takes place

riverbed | *prima materia* if I ever saw it, walked it, knew it, drank it

cross | bearer, bearing, born

icon | cottonwood leaves start as small hearts that grow large

vigil | parents call their friends to a feast one year after their
daughter dies

song | I cannot find the right key to begin

ripples | in which our separate dreams/prayers/recipes become
shared

gaze | wind picks up and disperses smoke across the valley

language | a surrogate mother whispering lullabies

signal | it won't be understood until too late but still it is made

veil | the forest burns and reveals earthen bones

12. ARRIVAL

Tears pool and burst from behind eyelids. *Reality,*
the Jungian analyst says gently, *is medicinal.*
But what part is real? Is this real? Is this? Is it?
The woman grounds herself after weeping,
prostrate upon dirt. The river is empty.
This is a desert: her skin envelops the ocean
within. Flowers are needed. Where can they
be found? Frost—it came too early. Why has
it come so early? His life ended in the forest
under a half moon in September. Like that,
the tide goes out. She jogs up the mountain,
weaving between ponderosas and rock.
Billowing clouds arrive, but could be plumes
of smoke as easily as cumulus bearing rain.

Walk In the Nambé Badlands

The sun has set.

In the long wait between rains,
     it is hot and very dry.

I walk through seven years of burning
and watch the badlands

     renew itself again and again.

Grasses unto grasses unto grasses.
I keep my head covered as if entering a temple.

I carry a ring of keys that are little
more than stems

     twisted into crosses,

and give birth without the midwife at my side.

Acknowledgments

Thank you to the editors of the following journals for giving these poems, sometimes in earlier or excerpted forms, a first home:

Kitchen Table Press: "Offering in the Name of the Dead"

Pasatiempo: "The Thin Line"

Poem-a-Day: "Far Country"

Quarterly West: "Night Being a Moonlit Ordeal"

Qwerty: "Field Apothecary," "The Search for the Golden Spike," "Mid-winter Reckoning"

Raleigh Review: "Repurposing"

Sycamore Review: "Because Envy Leads Us Where We Need to Go"

The title of "Loss is Magnified by Knowing Change" comes from a line in the essay, "What we Have" by Laura Paskus, originally published in the *Santa Fe Reporter*.

The lines "large shifts at unprecedented rates" and "In all of this there is room for grief" also come from that essay.

"I have of late, but wherefore I know not lost all my mirth, this goodly frame the earth seems to me a sterile promontory" is Hamlet via the musical Hair.

"My innumerable hands, the weight I bear with all of my arms" is attributed to Our Lady of Woodstock as recorded in *The Way of the Rose* by Clark Strand and Perdita Finn.

Thank you to Daniel Kraft, Barabara Rockman, and Béatrice Szymkowiak whom I turn to, poems in hand, again and again. It would have been very lonely without you.

Thank you to the Oaks, for firelight on dark nights.

Thank you to my daughters and my parents. You bless my life daily.

Elliot, you are my country, near and far. Thank you for every mile traveled, every plant gathered, every midnight word. This book is for you.

About the Author

KYCE BELLO was the inaugural winner of the Test Site Poetry Prize with her debut collection, *Refugia*, which also received the New Mexico/Arizona Book Award. Bello edited the award-winning anthology *The Return of the River*, a work of literary activism.